A
Sharpened
Dagger

A Short Story

Phil Scott Mayes

DEDICATION

This one's for you, Caleb CW. I wouldn't have written it without your encouragement, and I'd be a sad, lonely writer without your friendship.

A Sharpened Dagger

V ivid nightmares plagued Job Abrams for as long as he could remember. The doctor called them night terrors. As a kid, he could only run, hide, and survive the night. He got good at it, much better than his twin brother, Daniel. Oddly, it was the revelation that the monsters were real that finally gave Job courage. If they were real, then Job wasn't powerless. He could hurt real things. Real things bled. And if they bled, they could be killed. Unlike Daniel, Job took control. He went hunting in his sleep. That's when the Daggers found him.

Now, in the perpetual darkness of the Void with dozens of missions under his belt, an oily projectile zipped past in a near miss that split the air with a deafening crack. The black stubble on his head stood straight and his heart thumped against his sternum. He controlled his breathing and held his M4's green laser where the thin, fluttering skin of the demon's throat would soon be exposed. The beast reared up and coiled its six tentacles to send another volley of digested and packed human bone.

"Come on. Do it, you ugly bastard," he growled.

Demons were prideful beasts, and that was the only

reason Daggers ever stood a chance. A demon never called for backup until gravely wounded, and sometimes not even then, but if it used its hive mind to call reinforcements, they would appear by the hundreds. The task force had lost more than a few good Daggers that way.

Job watched the demon's movements, waiting for the moment its body would begin to lurch. The creature's head was that of a warthog with the flesh peeled off— bone streaked with dried blood and fatty tissue. Its tusks were adorned with a garland of human entrails that swung wildly with every flick of its snout.

It occurred to Job that Satan was a mad scientist. Jealous of the Holy Father's creative power, he vindictively disfigured His creation. That would make the Void, at best, a playground for his ghouls, and at worst, a training ground for his army.

The demon's body began forward, jerking like a whip's handle and setting its tentacles in motion. That's when its head rose, exposing Job's fist-sized target. He squeezed the trigger smoothly and sent a burst of 5.56 into the creature's throat. Ripples fanned out where each bullet punched through the hide and tore into the telneurum— its communication organ.

Its tentacles flailed wildly, sending the next round of projectiles astray, and Job recognized another opening. He fired rounds at the demon's joints and marched forward with weapon raised until its hind legs buckled. The moment it met the forest floor, Job slung the rifle, drew a wooden rod from its sheath, and sprinted to finish the monster.

As he raised the rod high, it lengthened, and in a swirl of black particles, the head of a broad axe appeared. He swung the weapon down, severing the tentacles like twigs from a tree. The demon twisted and let out a hissing type of growl that coated Job's face with blood and bits of masticated meat. It swung its head, bent on skewering Job. Face coated in blood, Job could taste the iron, could hear the beast's snorting, could feel the air stirring, but couldn't see the tusk careening toward his left flank.

It plunged into Job's side, snapping a rib before popping his lung. Its skull slammed into him and sent him tumbling across the clearing. Pressure built with each shallow breath. His ribs ached mercilessly, but it paled in comparison to the pain of the demon's tentacles coiling tightly around his legs, squeezing until he thought his calves would burst.

The surge of pain as his bones cracked forced thought entirely from Job's mind, immersing him in fleeting oblivion.

By the time he regained his wits, the demon stood over him. Job rolled his head and spied the cabin he'd come to raid. That was the mission: kill the demon sentry, retrieve the artifact, and beat feet. Job also spied his axe and reached for it, grasping desperately among the tendrils and twigs for the staff, the only weapon he possessed that had the power to truly kill a demon. The rifle was efficient, its range and firepower unmatched, but a demon would inevitably heal from any wound it inflicted.

The creature's jaws opened for a crushing bite, and Job's fingers closed over his staff. It shortened and swirled with black particles once more, the axe head becoming a sword blade that he thrust as deeply as he could into the demon's neck, sawing with every ounce of strength he could muster. Blood spurted and frothy pink bubbles appeared at the gashed windpipe. It gurgled, choking on its own blood, then collapsed sideways.

The demon sentry was defeated, but the mission was far from complete. Hot lightning shot through his legs and left side, reminding him of his powdered bones and punctured lung, but it was the

tentacles pulling his feet beneath the loosened earth that would keep him from the cabin.

He dragged the sword's edge across the tentacles' rubbery skin, and they tightened further, grinding the jagged shards of bone against his muscle. Job cried out and flopped to his back knowing there was only one way forward.

He sat up, grunting loudly through the stabbing pain in his ribs, and raised the wooden staff. Again, the particles swirled as the handle lengthened slightly, and when the conversion was complete, he gripped a hatchet in his right hand. He retrieved a stout twig from the ground and placed it between his teeth. Then, with the sheer madness of determination, he swung the hatchet straight through his left leg midway between knee and ankle. The fragment of tentacle that remained around his calf tightened reflexively, staunching the wound. The hatchet fell from his fingers as he fought unconsciousness, but he found the blade, raised it again in quaking hands.

His right leg blurred beneath his tears as he brought it down, but the swing lacked conviction. The lackluster chop bounced off the bone.

Before he could lose will, he chopped like a maniac, each hack weaker than the last. He lost count of his swings, and when he thought he couldn't swing again, the hatchet split the bone. One more swing and it was done. When Job's mania subsided, he felt an ironic gratitude for his tentacle tourniquets.

Returning the staff to its sheath, he rolled to his belly and rose onto his forearms. He repositioned the M4 to his back and fought through fatigue and agony as he high-crawled to the cabin with its dry-rot walls and crooked door. Behind him, trails of blood glistened like oil on the moonlit undergrowth. It was always midnight there, always bleak and hopeless.

Job dragged himself up to the stoop. The door was unlocked, scraping as it opened to reveal his objective lying unceremoniously on the old wood planks. At first, the artifact looked as ancient as it was—coated in thick dust that obscured its exact shape and details. It wasn't until he crawled closer that, he saw modern lines and a simple structure. It looked like a military-issued web belt, but from the pounding in his chest, he knew it was indeed The Belt of Truth. He prayed silently that the other Daggers had retrieved their pieces of the Armor of God; ultimate victory would require the complete set. Job grabbed the belt, shook off the dust, and stuffed it in his pack.

A shrieking chorus pinballed off the viny trees of the hellish wood.

Job dug frantically under the neck of his uniform and followed the gold chain to the five-inch cross that dangled at its end. The beams were round, a half-inch in diameter, and ornately carved with ancient script and decorative flairs. He pressed the button at the top of the cross, releasing a spring-loaded dagger that extended from the bottom.

Job glanced out the door. An arm with bright red spots on glossy black scales reached around the trunk of a nearby tree. A pair of yellow eyes peeked from behind the trunk, an infected glowing in the moonlight. Job's heart dropped when he noticed the others. Hundreds of them—climbing, creeping, leering. The forest was alive.

He looked regretfully at the dagger in his hand. "I hate this part." He took a breath. "All things in Christ!"

He sunk the dagger smoothly into his chest, between the ribs, and through his heart.

‹†›

Job gasped, bolted upright, grabbing his chest then his legs, which were still attached. No matter how many times he went in, he couldn't get used to the dual reality. The two monks assigned to pray over him during the mission rushed by candlelight to his bedside, offering him water and a pan for purging. The spirit's experience waging holy war in the Void was completely immersive.

They felt everything as if it happened in the waking world.

There were only two ways back from the Void alive: waking up in the real world or dying by cross pendant in the Void. Sometimes Daggers just woke up, pulling their spirit back to their body, but it almost always meant mission failure. Such wake-ups were rare, so most missions concluded with suicide by sacred pendant. It gave the Daggers control over their exit. You had to endure the pain of getting stabbed in the heart each and every time, but it beat not waking up at all.

Any spiritual death in the Void meant death to the body—flatlined in sleep. Those were the stakes.

"Anybody else back yet?" Job whispered, trying to catch his breath despite having two healthy lungs again. He sipped water and eyed the monks who nodded in unison.

"Okay…is anybody still out?"

The monks shook their heads.

"Oh, c'mon. I was the last one?" he asked in disbelief.

No response.

Job touched his bare feet to the cool concrete floor and the feeling surprised him, almost painfully so, like pins and needles. Though they'd never actually been gone, it was as if he stood on new feet just grown from his roughly-hewn stumps.

Seven years he'd lived in the bunker—a decommissioned Cold War shelter. Now, at twenty-four, he found its cool cement walls warm and homey.

Job hobbled stiffly toward the bunker's entrance. The

reinforced main door wasn't the only way in or out, there was also a web of escape tunnels the task force had carved into the mountain over the years. Though it had been almost a century since the Daggers' last real-world engagement, they knew Satan's influence had consumed the hearts and minds of people around the globe. The threat was ever present.

He pushed the heavy door aside and breathed the crisp mountain air. Light swelled from the horizon as daybreak approached, but the veil of night had yet to lift entirely. Job set out across the lot to the compound's main gate. Fresh air and exercise often flushed the Void's rotten aftertaste, and if that didn't work, a cup of coffee at the guard shack would do the trick.

The existence of the task force was one of the world's best kept secrets, but the existence of the bunker was no special mystery. According to public record, it had been converted into a monastery. Mechanical maintenance and food delivery were handled by outside companies, each vetted and monitored, and that part of the operation usually ran like clockwork. The head monk saw to that and was the public face of the operation.

Cover aside, security was still necessary, so the Dagger trainees worked rotations at the main gate. That morning, Job found Mike Winters pulling guard duty with Joey Chin. Mike stood to approach the food service truck, squinting at its high beams. Pursuant to their training, Joey stayed in the guard booth where Job slid behind him to pour a cup from the steaming pot.

"Morning, fella," Mike greeted. "Could you please shut

off your headlights like the sign says." After a beat, the headlights flicked off. "Running ahead of schedule this month?"

It wasn't the usual driver, but judging by the curious tilt of Mike's head, he'd already noticed.

"Yeah, soup kitchen cancelled this month," the driver said, projecting over the engine noise. "Said donations were good and they didn't have room. Insisted we deliver it here free of charge. I was in the area, so I came early."

Mike nodded the way he did most things: slowly. "Very thoughtful. If I could see your driver's license, I'll make this quick and painless so we can get that food inside."

The driver's hands disappeared, rummaging out of sight below the window. "I'm new to this route. What is this place?"

"A monastery."

"With armed security and razor wire?"

"They value their privacy. Can't be too careful nowadays." There was only so much chit-chat Job could take, so he patted Joey on the shoulder and whispered, "One o'clock. Rec room. Texas hold 'em ass-whooping. Invite Mike." Then he started back toward the bunker.

Job had walked no more than twenty feet when there was a brief rustling from behind followed by wet choking and what sounded like Joey's coffee running off the counter and onto the floor. Job spun to see Joey grabbing at his neck, eyes bulging as crimson ribbons of blood spurted through his fingers.

Fear punched Job in the chest as his gaze flicked to

where Mike was staring down the business end of a suppressor. His forehead ate the bullet, the top of his skull flapping back like a toupee in a gust of wind. He teetered for a second, then slumped as his legs collapsed.

Job sprinted to a large safe just inside the bunker door, swiped his thumb, and grabbed a short-barreled M4 and a Glock 19. He heard the driver rap twice on the cab's door. The man yelled, "Let's go, you."

Job punched the red button beside the safe, sounding the bunker's internal alarm. He chambered a round in the rifle and raced outside just in time to see a shirtless, skeletally-thin man trot from behind the guard shack carrying a combat knife, wet with what had to be Joey's blood. A crudely painted pentagram glistened red on the man's bare chest as he moved for the back of the truck.

Job raised his M4 but glanced over his shoulder as feet padded out of the bunker in double-time. When he returned forward, the gaunt man had disappeared.

"Hold your fire," Commander Solomon said, striding to Job's side as his fellow Daggers took position behind concrete barricades. "Job, I need a sitrep."

"Two-plus enemy combatants in a box truck. Mike and Joey are dead. Driver has a handgun, shirtless man, a knife."

Job watched as the driver exited the truck and slowly raised his hands, grinning like a fool.

"Permission to engage?" Job asked.

"Stand down, son. If this is who I think it is, Command will want him alive."

"Well, good morning, y'all," the man said. "Do you

welcome all your delivery drivers this way or is it just my lucky day?"

"You're no delivery driver," Job said, "but I can tell you're not Fallen. Which groupie gang are you with?"

"You guys *are* good. Daggers, eh?" the driver said with another shit-eating grin. "Satan's Angels. I'm honored to finally find y'all."

The driver took several steps toward the bunker, and Commander Solomon ordered him to halt. The driver continued anyway, even after a warning shot cracked past him into the truck's grill.

Solomon motioned for a Dagger named Hannah to follow as he moved cautiously toward the driver who seemed unfazed by their approach.

"Cover us," he ordered the group. "Halt and turn away from the sound of my voice! Do it. NOW!"

"Commander Ramesses sends his regards," the driver said, bringing his arms behind him.

Job shouted, "Gun!" as the man produced a silenced handgun from his waistband.

A cacophony of gunfire erupted from the barricades. Little explosions of meat, bone, and blood painted the truck a chunky red as the bullets cratered the driver's body. He collapsed, the gunfire ceased, and the team moved in.

Solomon kicked the handgun clear of the driver who had been dead since Job's bullet popped through his left eye and tumbled around inside his skull. He turned to check on Hannah who was pressing a hand against an expanding dark spot on her thigh.

"I'm hit, sir," she called. When Solomon began to turn back, she barked, "I'm good! Check the truck."

"Hannah's hit. Left leg," Solomon bellowed to the others as he moved ahead.

Job and three other Daggers converged on the truck with weapons trained on the door. They opened it to find boxes of food, a bag of onions, and two dead bodies—the actual delivery drivers. The gaunt man was nowhere to be found.

Job began to circle the truck. "Anything?" he asked Commander Solomon, who was checking the cab.

"Clear!" Solomon responded.

Job continued around, weapon at the ready. He stooped for a view of the undercarriage, expecting to see the gaunt man clinging to the chassis like some humanoid bat, but once again there was no sign of him. Job finished his lap around the truck and bent down once more. That's when he spied the gaunt man behind the three trainees at the bunker's entrance.

With strength that defied his apparent frailty, he buried his knife in the base of a kid's skull and grabbed the trainee's M4. He unloaded bursts into the two remaining trainees then targeted the exposed team who scrambled for cover behind the truck.

For some it was too late.

The gaunt man fired round after round, ducking below the concrete, and changing his position at intervals. Several of them shot randomly at the barricades as they moved, but none came close to hitting the shooter. On her back, Hannah scooted across the ground, pushing with her good leg. As she drew it up for another push, supersonic lead hit her knee so hard, Job thought it was blown off entirely. She bawled in pain then laid without movement. For a moment, she appeared to be dead, but it was not so.

Job watched as Hannah slid her handgun free from its holster, laying as still as possible, playing dead. Once it was firmly in her grasp, she sat upright, took aim, and pulled the trigger.

Her shot split the gaunt man's ear and smacked the concrete behind him, but his return fire entered through her cheek and obliterated the far side of her skull on its way out.

"Shit! Hannah!" Job yelled. He hung his head. "Dammit, you almost got that fucker…"

Behind the concrete, the gaunt man killed with impunity, landing lethal rounds on five Daggers. He even had time to reload with the extra magazine the trainee had carried.

The truck was terrible cover and Job knew it. Not only were their legs dancing in plain sight beneath the chassis, the truck's box and cab weren't very likely to stop a bullet from passing through.

Job watched on as Solomon chanced a glimpse through the cab's windows and recoiled as the glass burst with a loud snap. The commander turned to them. "We have numbers, but he has position. We have to split up. Storm from both sides of the truck. One team should get a clear shot while he's focused on the other. Job, take Zeke. Naomi, on me."

"Wait. Sir, do you have a full mag?" Job asked, and Solomon nodded. Job laid prone, using the truck's back tires as cover. "Shoot through the truck's cab to draw his attention."

Solomon reached the weapon into the window's opening, aimed in the direction of the bunker, and held the trigger down. Job rolled out from behind the wheels, took aim, and fired one shot through the gaunt man's head.

‹ † ›

Ramesses leaned against the fender of the Mercedes SUV watching his lieutenant, Crezik, and the rest of his four-man strike team load the Gulfstream with rifle cases and ammo cans. Ramesses took another drag from his cigarette; they had eliminated prayer groups, potential Dagger trainees, and even Void scouts, but they'd never had an opportunity like this. Victory at Mount Esther wouldn't end the war, but it would be monumental. After the bunker, they could begin hunting the young ones.

‹ † ›

"The Fallen will send a team before we can relocate or reinforce our ranks," Commander Solomon said, then paused before gravely predicting, "They're probably already on their way."

Solomon stared at the tortured souls that, like Job, had become their only family. "We've never been this close to the full Armor of God. We have to go in tonight—one final push for the sword."

Naomi raised a hand. "Shouldn't we defend the bunker?"

"We will, but the bunker is lost. Tomorrow, we'll move on and by the time we're settled into the new location, the Sword of the Spirit will be gone. It could take the scouts centuries to find it again. Zeke, you'll come with Job, Naomi, and me. The others will play defense."

"I've never seen combat before," Zeke noted nervously.

"This operation was going to be tough with a full team of seven. Without you,"—Solomon scanned the stale briefing room, and Job knew the commander saw the same thing he did: peaceful monks and pubescent youths—"we'll only have three. We need you, son, and I think you're ready."

Zeke stared downward and nodded with growing conviction. "Okay, let's do this."

They spent the day preparing their bodies for sleep with hard labor and intense training. At least a full hour before sunset, the task force convened one last time to reiterate the plan before heading to their individual alcoves. Job entered the candlelit space and slugged the sleep tea that the monks prepared. He laid staring at the ceiling before closing his eyes with a prayer and achieving a state of repetitive thought that lulled him to sleep.

He soon found himself back in the hellish wilderness. Though the sun still warmed the west peak of Mount

Esther, it was vacuously dark within the Void. The only light was a dull glow that seemed to emanate from the air itself. He stood on a riverbed checking his gear as he awaited the others.

The Void was a half-step between the human plane and hell and wasn't meant to host the human spirit. It was a demonic space even the Daggers didn't fully understand. After centuries of operation, they knew little more than it contained hideous beasts that fed on humanity, and that those beasts could be killed.

Their ultimate target was an apocalyptic harbinger called the Abomination of Desolation, a creature of horrifying repute—the bastard mutant of hell's grief and torment. It was the head of the serpent, ripe for removal, but that would be impossible without the full Armor of God.

The stones beside him jostled, and when he looked, Solomon stood there.

"Just us so far?" the commander asked.

"So far," replied Job. "Hopefully Zeke finds us without trouble. I don't like his chances alone."

Naomi materialized in knee deep water and looked down with disappointment. "Insertions: never an exact science," she quipped as she stepped onto dry land. "Still waiting on Zeke?"

"Yeah, I already checked my gear," said Job. "Wouldn't mind a buddy check though."

Before Naomi could do so, the wall of tropical greenery rustled behind them, and they immediately spun and aimed their M4s. Their fingers rested on their triggers as the movement drew closer. The leaves shook violently, and Zeke plowed through, coming to an abrupt halt with his hands raised.

"Damn, Zeke. You almost got lit up," Naomi shouted.

"Missed the insertion point. Sorry."

"You'll get better with practice," Solomon said. "Let's get situated.

That rise behind Naomi needs to stay on our left. Zeke, the jagged ridge behind you—"

Solomon trailed off, as dumbstruck as Job. The bald hill that was behind Naomi just moments before had been replaced by the jagged ridge he expected to see behind Zeke. Even the river flowed the opposite direction, though none of them had changed positions.

"You saw the hill behind Naomi, right?"

"A-firm," replied Job. They looked that way again and beheld the jagged ridge, then looked behind Zeke and saw the smooth rise that had been behind Naomi.

"It's reconfiguring to disorient us," Solomon said.

"It's working," Naomi muttered. "How are we supposed to navigate when the landscape keeps shifting?"

"The temple is along this river," Job said. "We could split up and go opposite directions. That, or we all pick a direction and hope for the best."

Naomi shook her head. "Splitting up helps our chances of finding the temple, but if we cross an alpha-class demon or the Abomination itself when there's only two of us..."

"Job's right," Solomon said firmly. "We have split up. Teams of two. We need the sword. Fight hard and remember your training. Punching out is a last resort."

Job grabbed Naomi and Zeke's shoulders, making eye contact with each before looking at Solomon. "All things in Christ."

"He gives us strength," they said in unison.

"Before we split," Solomon started as he dug through his pack and tossed item after item to Job, "you need to put the armor on."

"Me?"

"The monks had a vision. You need to wear it."

As much as Job wanted to argue, there was no time. He donned the Boots of Readiness, Breastplate of Righteousness, Shield of Faith, Helmet of Salvation, and Belt of Truth. Armored up, he looked like a special forces operator complete with body armor, combat boots, and ballistic helmet. Wearing it centuries ago would've made him look like a medieval knight, but the eternal armor changed to suit contemporary warfare.

Solomon headed off with Zeke, Job with Naomi, setting out in opposite directions. Hiking the riverbank offered ease of passage, but there was no cover, and every puff of moldy air stirred the walls of lush greenery on each side of them, revealing eyes that tracked their every move.

The jungle watched.

Maintaining their footing was difficult. The ground seemed to rise and fall with each step, as though they treaded the chest of a sleeping giant. This was not the Void Job knew. This was the umbilic epicenter through which the malignancy of hell transfused.

Black serpents slithered up a nearby tree, twisting around and through each other to become a noose that hung low from an overhead branch. It wiggled stiffly before them as an accusation wheezed within Job's mind. His twin brother also had the gift, but the terrors broke him at a young age. Substance abuse, depression, and schizophrenia followed. A little over a year ago, Job visited him during leave and saw his brother's hopelessness. The final night of his visit, Job had woken in a cold sweat and went for a drink of water. He had found his brother hanging from a rafter in the kitchen, face purple, eyes wide and bulging.

As far as Job was concerned, his brother had been dead since he found him with that extension cord cinched tightly around his neck. His parents, however, refused to let him go and had kept him on life support ever since.

The noose of serpents was a sadistic ploy to summon that pain, and Naomi could see it on Job's face. She stepped forward and drew her staff with a twirl, producing a katana blade from the cloud of black dust.

"Don't," Job warned. "I don't want to pick a fight we don't have to."

"It bothers me that it knows we're here but *it's* not picking a fight with us."

"Me too. It's like it's waiting for something."

‹†›

Crezik and his team quickly loaded their gear into the Land Rover. Vigrim, the team's youngest member and best driver, took the wheel and peeled out of the lot toward the foothills of Mount Esther as Crezik briefed the mission one final time.

The concept was clear even if the details were lacking. Their gaunt assassin would have found one of the bunker escape tunnels and disabled whatever security existed, then attacked while the task force was distracted. The exact number of Daggers remaining was unknown, but Crezik and Ramesses knew the assassin would exceed expectations. They would infiltrate the bunker via the escape tunnel and quietly lay waste to everyone inside. It was a simple plan, but their enemy's complacency made it effective.

Crezik eyed the distant peak of Mount Esther and offered a prayer to the dark lord of hell. If Satan would delay attacking the Daggers in the Void, the Fallen could kill their sleeping bodies.

‹†›

Solomon and Zeke trekked along the stony riverbed, sensing the malevolent life beneath their boots. The air smelled and felt like steam rising from a corpse. Only seventeen, this was Zeke's first experience in the jungle, but no earthly jungle could've prepared him for this.

Bile floated in his esophagus, threatening to erupt without warning. "I don't feel good, sir."

"That's normal. It gets easier with time. In a few operations you'll barely notice."

"*If* there's another operation," Zeke muttered. "I've

got a bad feeling."

"Sense of doom is also normal. You'll get used to it." Solomon clapped Zeke on the shoulder, but the commander looked as green as Zeke felt. Seemed more on edge, too.

Zeke's next step brought the thin crunch of a trampled eggshell. Where he'd stepped, a black rock had shattered leaving a gooey pink puddle. He knew exactly what it was and heaved violently.

"No, no, no," Zeke whimpered between bouts of retching.

"What's wrong?"

Zeke looked at Solomon with tearful, self-loathing. "It's a fetus."

"A *human* fetus?" Solomon asked in horror. He looked back at the pink puddle.

Zeke nodded, out of breath and riding the frothy lip of another heave. "It's my sister."

"That's not your sister, Zeke. The void is messing wi—"

A branch cracked loudly. Then another. Leaves in the surrounding trees swished violently.

A woman in tattered rags stood before them on the riverbed, silhouetted by the meager light's reflection off the turbulent waters. Her features were blanked out by shadow, and she breathed with a heavy rattle. She stood frozen, eyes locked on the fetus in existential devastation. Over the tranquil babbling of the water, she began to sob and step mechanically toward the crushed remains.

She lowered herself onto all fours, nearly burying her

face in the viscous mass. In a guttural, shrieking timbre, she cried, "You killed her, Zeke!"

Zeke wept as he stumbled toward the woman.

"Zeke, stop!" barked Solomon, but Zeke was lost in a memory. His parents loomed over him, aged eight, yelling. It had been a tragic accident, but he felt deserving of their vitriol. He had killed his unborn sister. Despite numerous lectures, he had again left his toy trucks at the top of the staircase. This time, his six-months-pregnant mother had tripped over them while carrying the laundry basket. The fall down the stairs destroyed her baby and any hope of having another.

"Zeke!" Solomon's voice sounded very far away.

His mother abruptly stopped crying. She turned to face Zeke. Her tears were black tar, her eyes blacker still. "It's your fault she's dead! It's your fault I'm in this hell!"

She pounced on Zeke, knocking him to the ground. Two sharp reports sounded and the creature's head, that of Zeke's mother, popped like a water balloon. Her skin peeled back and dumped her foul, liquified insides all over him.

Zeke spat the gore from him as the demon fell away. "It got in my mouth!" He spat again. "What the hell is happening?"

"Hell is exactly what's happening," Solomon said. "The Void is toying with us." The commander helped Zeke up, sighed in sympathy when he looked him over. "I'm sorry, son, but we need to keep moving. Are you okay?"

Zeke nodded and washed up in the river. The water

was downright hot, turning his hands redder with each subsequent dip.

He stood on rubbery legs, glanced at the broken rock and squashed unborn child, and felt something crawl inside of him.

‹ † ›

Crezik's team bumped through the towering aspens to a small clearing far enough back to avoid detection. They geared up and hiked through the alpine forest until only a low mound and cluster of trees stood between them and the bunker. At night, it looked like it was a part of the mountain, blending into its rocky face.

They picked up their assassin's trail in the fallen pine straw and tracked it over the hill from the bunker's entrance, finding an exposed metal hatch where the dirt was swept away. Carefully, they pried up on the hatch. No traps or alarms. One at a time, they crawled through the narrow tunnel.

They were inside.

‹ † ›

Shadows swayed ahead. Someone, some*thing*, was moving toward them. Job and Naomi froze. The shadows froze too. For a long, terrifying second, Job and Naomi stood rigidly still, staring into the darkness. Job had the unnerving thought that were looking at their own evil reflections. They dropped to a knee in unison and raised their weapons, painting the figures with their lasers.

The shadows did the same. Job's heart beat loudly in his ears. He tightened his grip and aimed between the target's collarbones. The laser deflected off something shiny. A chain like the one he wore, the one given only to Daggers.

"Identify yourself," Job ordered.

Solomon's familiar voice called out for them to hold their fire, bringing Job a wave of relief that was followed immediately by foreboding. "What are you doing here? You should be miles away."

"We went opposite directions and never turned back," answered Solomon, his frown deepening. "This is impossible."

Job finally got close enough to see that Zeke was a mess. "What happened to him?"

Zeke's eyes were bleeding, he was sweating profusely—sweat tainted with blood—and he was shivering with fever. The kid doubled over with a coughing fit that soaked his hand red. Solomon shook his head at Job and Naomi; Zeke wouldn't survive.

They laid him on his back and warned him of the pain he would experience, assuring him that he'd awaken safe and sound in the bunker. Even with their reassurances, Zeke's face registered absolute terror as Solomon withdrew Zeke's pendant and released the blade. Despite his whimpered pleading, Job and Naomi held his arms down.

"It's going to be okay, Zeke," Naomi said.

Solomon raised the dagger, and Zeke's eyes grew wide

with fear and panic as the commander drove the blade into the kid's heart.

‹ † ›

Zeke awoke projectile vomiting, and the monks rolled him onto his side. He pushed them away and struggled out of the bed. "I need some air, but I have to go back," he panted. "A demon was right behind Naomi."

He hit the door release button and stepped into the eerily silent corridor.

There was blood on the cement floor.

At first it was just a few drops, but as he edged toward the common area, the drops became a trail. His heart pounded in his eardrums. Glancing from the end of the hallway, he saw the trail grow thicker in the direction of the chow hall. Zeke snuck to the armory, grabbed a vest and rifle, and emerged, peering through the holographic optic.

He posted up against the cafeteria wall and listened. The faint odor of urine, feces, and iron that permeated the air had grown potent, almost flavorful, and as it wafted into his nostrils he couldn't help hacking. He heard jostling and a muffled wail and turned the corner ready to fire, but before he could even register his targets, a shattering pain exploded in his right shoulder as a bullet cleaved the joint in two. The M4 hung from its sling and Zeke watched helplessly as a clean-cut man finished gutting his friend Jacob. They tossed the trainee, entrails dragging beneath him, onto the pile of bodies in the corner.

The Fallen were here, just as Commander Solomon predicted.

Another shot rang out, and pain ripped through Zeke's other shoulder, then both knees. Zeke dropped, yelled in agony as he tried to move. The shooter stood over him and tilted his head inquisitively.

"I really hope you aren't just another trainee," the man said, pointing a bloodied knife.

Zeke responded in the way he thought might earn mercy, or at least make him valuable. "I'm...a Dagger," he said, fighting through the monstrous pain in his arms and legs. "Just got promoted."

The shooter's lips spread into a sinister grin. "Congratulations."

He cut off Zeke's index finger then slashed his throat. Zeke lay there squirming, each pulse sending a warm gush onto his chest.

"We're in," the shooter said, smiling cheerfully and holding up the finger.

Zeke's vision started to narrow.

Another Fallen stepped over Zeke and snatched the finger. Two more blurred figures followed.

A dull ringing sharpened in Zeke's ears, but he still heard one of them say, "The alcoves are this way."

Zeke's head rolled to the side, each painful heartbeat more sluggish than the last. He watched through fading vision as the dark shapes moved toward the alcove hallway. Delirium scrambled his mind, but two thoughts came clearly. His finger was programmed into the scanners. It was the key they needed to slaughter his family.

A single tear fell from Zeke's nose onto the concrete as numbness set in.

His world went black.

‹ † ›

The beast's jaws clamped down on Naomi's head, ripping it messily from her shoulders. Job and Solomon fired a volley of rounds from their M4s that had the wolf-like creature take a defensive stance. It stood nearly ten feet at its withers and had large flaps of scaly hide that laid forward from its neck, shielding its head. It looked canine, but its snout split vertically so that it splayed open four ways. Long barbs extended from its spine, the flesh over its ribs stripped away, revealing pitted and decaying bones.

When the men ceased fire, the scales that covered the demon's head bloomed outward like reptilian neck frills that shuddered as it roared. Job glanced to where Naomi's headless body still pumped blood onto the river's edge.

"Keep it occupied," Job snarled.

Solomon nodded, switched out magazines, then fired short bursts at the demon's head. It covered up again and shrunk back, exposing the telneurum at the base of its skull. Solomon targeted it while Job flanked to the beast's left. He slung his rifle and brandished his staff which lengthened in his hands to form a pike. Sprinting at the demon's side, he aimed the spear behind the shoulder blade, but the beast sensed his approach and razor-sharp ribs sprung outward, nearly impaling Job.

He slid under the demon's belly and, in one swift motion, thrust the pike through its heart and out the other side of its body. Job rolled clear as the creature slammed to the ground.

Commander Solomon approached Job, helped him to his feet, then yanked the pike from the demon's carcass and handed it to him. Without a word, Solomon went to Naomi's body, and Job followed. He knelt as Solomon said a prayer over Naomi then collected her pendant. Rather than follow the river they decided to climb the bald hill, hoping to determine the temple's actual location. Turning their staffs to machetes, they chopped their way through the jungle to the clearing where the hill rose before them. Then they climbed.

As naked as he felt during the climb, and as vulnerable as they were at the summit, Job took the fact that they hadn't been attacked as a bad omen. Passage through the Void was never freely given. From the top they could see the temple in the valley below. It resembled a Mayan pyramid and glowed with a foul green ambiance. They didn't speak as they descended the hillside, said nothing as they braved the jungle again, but as they neared the temple, Job's sickness intensified and the atmosphere grew thick, making sight and breath a labor.

With every step, the jungle watched. Waited.

It was the waiting that concerned Job the most.

‹ † ›

There were four doors on each side of the alcove hall. Some bore nameplates. After Zeke's, the Fallen entered the door labeled *'Naomi'* to find a pair of monks praying over her lifeless body.

The monks died easily.

On the way out, Vigram stabbed Naomi's corpse for good measure.

The next two rooms were empty. Only two remained.

‹ † ›

Job and Solomon reached the edge of the jungle and gazed upon the base of the pyramid. Burning torches formed a perimeter and lined each side of the staircase that ascended its face, but their flames flickered with an infected green. Job wondered if, with every breath, he sucked disease into his lungs.

Weapons shouldered, they moved into the clearing, rifles sweeping left and right in search of threats as they crept toward the temple's steps. They reached the pyramid's base, crouched low between the flickering torches. There was something in the sound of the flames, and at the edge of his hearing, Job could make out one word, chanted: des-o-la-tion.

Solomon's gaze snapped to Job, his eyes wild with fear. "We need that sword—now!"

Job bolted, but the moment Job's boot landed on the temple stairs, the entire jungle exploded in a blistering scream. Branches and leaves whipped violently, and both men startled at the unexpected sound—a scream that was not just one voice but billions coming together in a shrieking wail they could feel in their bones. The Abomination of hell had arrived.

They sprinted toward the pyramid's peak without hazarding a look back. At the top, they spun with rifles raised and hearts drubbing. It stood there in the torches' unnatural light, a grotesque behemoth beyond their darkest imaginings.

Almost twenty feet tall, it was bipedal and vaguely human in form, but only in the most macabre sense. Six human arms jutted from around its head like the points of a royal crown, their fingers stripped to the bone and splayed outward like antlers. Atop its bulbous head was a dense mop of blood vessels and veins that flowed like hair down to its shoulders. Black, stippled flesh was stretched tightly over its head, torn in several places revealing a patchwork skull with jagged, bloody seams.

It had hollow impressions where eyes would normally be and two small cavities in place of a nose. Only its mouth was clearly defined, but it was a lipless chasm, disproportionately large with several rows of razor-sharp teeth.

"Go find the sword. I'll hold it off," Solomon ordered. His somber expression made it clear that this was his last stand; there would be no punching out.

With a nod, Job rushed into the temple's interior as the Abomination levitated up the steps. Like it had in the presence of the belt, Job's pulse quickened as he drew nearer to the sword. When gunfire sounded behind him, he sprinted down corridors, checking rooms along the way until he found it.

The Sword of the Spirit.

It wasn't what he expected. It was identical in shape and size to the staff he wore on his hip, but as he picked up the sword, the balance and efficiency of the weapon were perfection. The grip was a dark gray metal with decorative etching and gold inlay. Its beauty made him smile.

He rushed back to the temple's entrance, confident in their imminent victory over the Abomination and eager to see it finished. He reached the door just in time to see the meat fall from Solomon's bones like clumps of snow from a tree. The commander's bones then dried to dust, crumbling and blowing away to become a part of the Void's everlasting terrain.

‹ † ›

Crezik wiped the blood from his knife and lifted his boot clear of the expanding red pool. The door read: *'Commander Solomon'*. They were nearly finished with their good work.

"Wonder what that looked like inside the Void," mused Vigrim.

"What *what* looked like?" Brigner asked.

"When Crezik killed him, I wonder what happened to his spirit in the Void."

Crezik lunged and put his knife blade against Vigrim's jugular.

"Stay focused, boy. We're not done yet."

‹ † ›

Job had never seen anything like Solomon's death. Grief compelled Job to Solomon's remains. He knelt, holding the Sword of the Spirit's bladeless handle, scanned the surroundings, but didn't see the Abomination anywhere.

Turning back, he was struck in the chest by a whipping appendage. Airborne and falling backward off the temple's two-hundred-foot peak, he spied the Abomination standing atop the entrance roof, tucking a bony tail back out of sight. Freefalling, Job braced, fully expecting the impact to kill him, but when he hit the ground, it felt cushioned.

The Armor of God.

When he saw the Abomination's stinger broken off in the armor plate, he knew it had protected him. The pointed shard of bone was lodged deep, but he wiggled it free and tossed it behind him. Where it landed, the ground turned black and bubbled, and the stinger dissolved into the tar.

Job drew the Sword of the Spirit, twirling it as he would his own staff, and a broadsword materialized in a cloud of white-hot sparks. It was lightweight, perfectly balanced and engulfed with a rippling flame. He gazed up the pyramid as the Abomination floated down the stairs with its four arms stretching stiffly outward.

Then he felt the knife.

‹ † ›

Crezik loomed over the last of the sleeping Daggers, the cool stone walls still warm with the blood of slain monks.

Glancing back at the door he read aloud, "Job."

He watched Job's eyes flick around beneath their veiny lids and wondered what cosmic battle was being waged inside the Void. Crezik wished he had the Daggers' gift, wished that in killing Job, he could inherit it.

Sending his men from the room, Crezik knelt by the bed, closed his eyes, and whispered a prayer to Satan. Boldly, he asked that he might be blessed enough to enter the Void, to gaze upon the dark lord's magnificence as a reward for his obedience. Then he stood, cycled a cleansing breath, and stabbed Job in the head with enough force to send the blade's tip crunching into the cot below.

‹ † ›

Job felt it the moment the blade entered his body's forehead, slicing open the hemispheres of his brain and releasing a fatal flood. In the Void it was a shooting pain that faded as quickly as it came, but afterward he felt hollowed out. He was a decal, peeled from his backing and stuck to the fabric of the Void. His body was dead, but his spirit remained; whether sustained by the protection of the armor or some other quality knitted into his being, he didn't know.

As the Abomination reached the ground, the skeletal

fingers atop its crown of arms curled in waves, producing a black spark that grew to an empty flame above its head. The behemoth drew back and spewed scalding tar from its gaping mouth. Job dropped to a knee and extended his forearm before him. The Shield of Faith materialized from the cuff like a shimmering hologram, blocking the hellfire. He shook its venom from the shield, then stood to attack but the Abomination was only inches away.

Its four massive arms gripped Job with serpentine fingers and lifted him high. As Job's face approached the empty flame at the center of the demon's crown, he felt no heat and realized it wasn't a flame but a gateway. He had no intention of discovering what lay the other side. The crown of arms grabbed Job's helmet and neck, attempted to drag him into the gateway, but the Helmet of Salvation sparked like a grinding wheel, preventing his passage. It didn't prevent the flashes of hell on the other side. The crown kept pulling and the sparking swelled with blinding intensity until a small explosion blew the crown of arms to pieces, extinguishing the gateway and sending Job tumbling.

The jungle whipped and screamed. The creature shrieked as it stepped back. Power surged not just through the armor and the sword, but through Job's body. Calling on the Boots of Readiness, he pushed against the spongy soil, sprinting straight at the Abomination with impossible speed. He jumped and planted both boots in its chest, launching it back against the temple stairs that cracked upon impact.

Job marched at the Abomination, the sword crackling

with flame. He raised it to strike, but the Abomination whipped its tail—a chain of meat and bones like an elephant's spine—to block the attack. The sword sliced smoothly through the tail and severed two of the demon's large arms. Tar-like blood splashed into Job's eyes. It burned like acid, and he tried to wipe it away, but it had merged with his flesh, welding his eyelids shut.

Job was blind.

He heard the Abomination moving to strike and strained against the tar to peel his eyes open. Raw power surged through them, and they burst into flames, melting away the tar. The beast lurched upright, jaws open and razor teeth exposed.

Job sidestepped the first attack and then another. He dove, rolled right, gained position behind the Abomination. It wore a collar of human heads, their bare spines hanging like a shredded cape. They melded with its shoulders and were animated as if still alive. The faces wept, muddy tears running down their cheeks.

Job sunk the Sword of the Spirit into the demon's back. Then again. And again. He wound up to slice the monster in two but it collapsed, face to the earth. The ground beneath it turned black and began to bubble. It sunk slowly until it was swallowed completely. The bubbling settled and the black stain shrank as if draining into a cavern below.

A convulsive clamor arose from the jungle. Branches cracked, tree trunks bent, and leaves flapped furiously amid a chorus of growling, hissing, and screeching. Job remembered the horde of demons that approached when he took the Belt of Truth and, despite his confidence in the armor, wouldn't chance a battle against such numbers.

Job meditated. As he did, a thread snaked through his grey matter. His mind was reconfiguring, new connections forming. It wove a web of revelation. He knew the Armor of God as if he had crafted it himself. Knew the capabilities of each piece. Knew what he needed to do next. He turned toward the jungle, held the sword aloft, then plunged it into the dirt blade-first.

The ground cracked outward in branching bolts that glowed with a holy fire. It spread from his location in a shockwave that set the jungle ablaze. The inferno towered on all sides of the temple clearing, and though its heat should've cooked him alive, he found its radiance refreshing.

"That's for my family!" Job yelled. "For the Daggers and...my brother!"

As the fire raged on, he plopped onto the temple's steps, inspected the sword, and enjoyed the chorus of screaming demons.

"How the hell am I gonna get out of this one?"

Like his namesake, Job had lost everything, and the Holy Father had allowed it. His body was dead, the people who had become his family were undoubtedly dead, the bunker that had become his home was surely destroyed, and it'd be a miracle if he ever found a way back to the waking world. Still, the Holy Father had preserved his spirit and entrusted him with great power, and that was all the evidence of the Lord's goodness that Job required.

He didn't believe the Abomination to be vanquished and had no interest in staying at that temple for all eternity. Death would be better. Job held his cross pendant and prayed for a miracle, mustering absolute conviction in its delivery. It rested heavily in his hand as he released the blade.

"One last poke to get me woke. Or not."

‹ † ›

There was a quiet beep. Then another.

Something was wrapped around his arms, and he couldn't pull air into his lungs. Job's eyes sprung open. He was alive and in a hospital. Panicked, he pulled and gagged at the tube in his throat. He tried to sit up, but a nurse charged into the room and gently pushed him back, telling him to slow down. Two more nurses rushed in to assist the first as they took vitals and tended to him.

Something was in his hand.

The Sword of the Spirit's handle rested at his side, wrapped in his fingers.

"You've been out a while. It's quite a miracle you're even here, to be honest," a nurse said.

His body felt strong though, and he had spent enough time in bed. Job stood, almost shoving the nurse aside in the process.

"Sir, you need to stay calm. Please, lay back down and let us run some tests first." Job headed for the door instead. "Daniel!" barked the nurse.

Job stopped, his heart thumping. "What did you call

me?"

"Your name. Daniel."

Job raced to the bathroom, locked the door behind him, and untied the knot at the back of his neck. The hospital gown fell to the floor and as he stepped in front of the mirror, a reflection slid into view that would've been his if not for the short beard and chest tattoo.

They were his twin brother's.

Remembering that he still held the staff, he gave it a twirl and the blade appeared in a shower of sparks. His face glowed hot with its radiance. Looking past the sword to his new reflection, he saw his spirit clad in the Armor of God with black-ringed eyes of fire that nearly startled him.

The Fallen had won the battle, but Job would win the war.

ACKNOWLEDGEMENTS

This short story was originally published in the military action-horror anthology SNAFU: Holy War. I must, therefore, start by thanking AJ Spedding and Geoff Brown at Cohesion Press. Your belief in this tale and diligence in its refinement are responsible not only for its polish, but for the tremendous growth I experienced throughout the process. I am thrilled to be a part of the SNAFU universe and wish you all continued success with your publications!

There are many people who laid eyes on this story and provided feedback from inception to submission. Foremost, I want to thank my dear friends and fellow authors Darynda Jones and Caleb CW for your expert guidance and cherished companionship. I also want to thank Gerry, Aaron, and Thomas for beta reading and sharing your invaluable notes. Finally, I must thank all of my good friends in the Portales writers' group. You are a network of wonderful writers and enjoyable people whose support has preserved my sanity on many occasions. I am better for having known each of you, and I have missed you terribly since I moved away.

ABOUT THE AUTHOR

Phil Scott Mayes is the author of Verity Rising and A Sharpened Dagger. An avid fan of horror and thriller genres, his works are down-to-earth, relatable, and gritty interpretations of supernatural and science fiction themes. He sees each tale as an opportunity to explore meaningful questions and challenge readers—or at least himself—with new ideas.

Phil has served in the Air Force Reserve and has earned an avionics degree from the Community College of the Air Force and a B.S. in organizational management from Spring Arbor University. He has traveled the world, worked a wide range of jobs, discovered a wide range of interests, and now wants nothing more than to stay at home crafting stories and spending time with family.

He was born and raised in Michigan where he now resides with his wife and three children.